FRIENDS
OF ACPL

W9-BAY-009

MARILKA

STORY AND PICTURES BY JANINA DOMANSKA

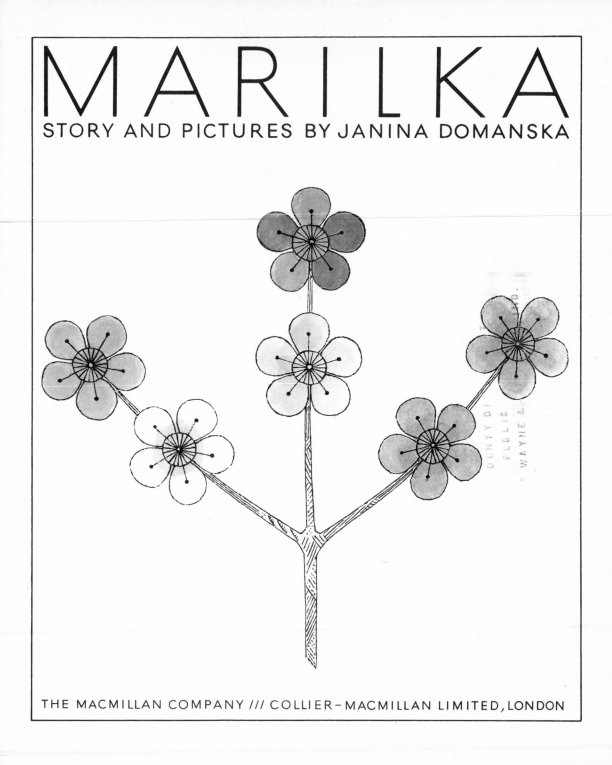

THE MACMILLAN COMPANY /// COLLIER–MACMILLAN LIMITED, LONDON

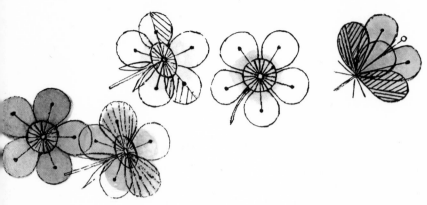

Copyright © Janina Domanska 1970. Printed in the United States of America. All rights reserved. No part of this book may be reproduced or transmitted in any form or by any means, electronic or mechanical, including photocopying, recording or by any information storage and retrieval system, without permission in writing from the Publisher. The Macmillan Company, 866 Third Avenue, New York, New York 10022. Collier-Macmillan Canada Ltd., Toronto, Ontario. Library of Congress catalog card number: 79-101729.

FIRST PRINTING

To Witold, Anna and Andrew

CO. SCHOOLS
C757752

Marilka was not home.

er parents looked for their little girl.

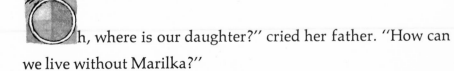h, where is our daughter?" cried her father. "How can we live without Marilka?"

When the stork heard these good people crying, he began to pull out his wing feathers.

"Marilka is lost. Her mother is crying, her father is crying. I don't want to fly anymore," he said, and started to sob.

he cherry tree saw the stork's feathers floating by and asked what was happening. When the stork replied, the cherry tree began to shake with grief. All its blossoms fell off and blew away. "I don't want to grow any more cherries now that Marilka is lost," it cried.

The river saw the cherry blossoms flying in the wind, and asked the tree what had happened.

"Ooo . . . oo . . . oo," moaned the cherry tree. "Marilka is lost. Her mother is crying, her father is crying, the stork has pulled out his feathers, and I have shaken off all my blossoms."

"Oh!" groaned the river. "What shall we do?"

t began to ripple and sigh until its waters overflowed and sank into the earth. Soon it was just a little stream.

Magda the goose girl came to fill her pitcher and let her goslings swim in the river. When she saw that it had become a stream, she was so surprised she dropped the pitcher, and it broke into little pieces.

h, River, what has happened to you?" she asked, while the goslings quacked all around her.

"Ooo . . . oo," cried the river. "Marilka is lost. I don't want to be a river anymore." And it continued to gurgle and ripple and get smaller and smaller.

h my, oh my!" cried Magda. She sat down among the broken pieces of the pitcher, while her goslings went off to look for another place to swim.

anek, a young shepherd, came to see Magda. He played her a song on his flute. When the goose girl told him what had happened, he stopped playing at once. "What terrible news," he cried. "What shall we do without Marilka?"

ust then one of the lambs came up. "Please, Master," he said, "don't stop playing. The grass tastes better when you play."

"I am too unhappy," said Janek. "Marilka is lost. Her mother and father are crying, the stork has pulled out his feathers, the cherry tree has shaken off its blossoms, the river has turned into a stream, Magda has broken her pitcher and the goslings have gone away."

CO. SCHOOLS
C757752

The lamb shook his head. "Marilka is not lost," he said. "She took the goat to the pasture as she does every morning. Look, here she comes now."

When everybody saw Marilka, her parents laughed with joy, the stork grew new feathers, the cherry tree covered itself with fresh blossoms, the stream became a river again, Magda fetched a new pitcher for water, and the goslings came waddling back. Janek sat down and played a gay tune while the lambs ate the grass which had never tasted better.

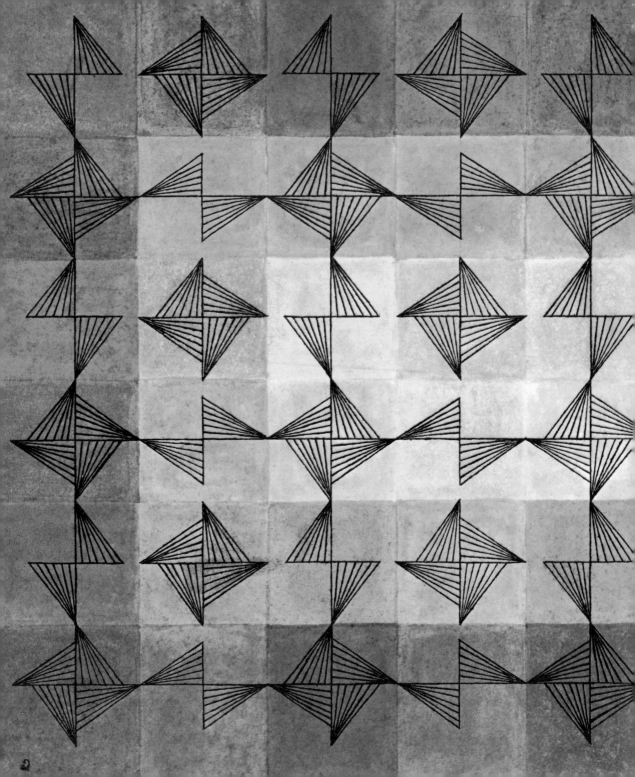